KANGAROO STEW

BY ZAC JAMES

This is a Magabala Book

LEADING PUBLISHER OF ABORIGINAL AND TORRES STRAIT ISLANDER STORYTELLERS.

CHANGING THE WORLD, ONE STORY AT A TIME.

First published 2024
Magabala Books Aboriginal Corporation
1 Bagot Street, Broome, Western Australia
Website: www.magabala.com
Email: sales@magabala.com

Magabala Books is assisted by the Australian Government through Creative Australia, its principal arts investment and advisory body. The State of Western Australia has made an investment in this project through the Department of Local Government, Sports and Cultural Industries.

Magabala Books is Australia's leading independent Aboriginal and Torres Strait Islander publishing house. Magabala Books acknowledges the Traditional Owners of the Country on which we live and work. We recognise the unbroken connection to traditional lands, waters and cultures. Through what we publish, we honour all our Elders, peoples and stories, past, present and future.

Cover design by Gene Eaton, Magabala Books

Typeset by Post Pre-press

Printed by Griffin Press, South Australia

ISBN 978-1-922777-12-6 (Print)
ISBN 978-1-922777-14-0 (ePDF)
ISBN 978-1-922777-15-7 (EPUB)

A catalogue record for this book is available from the National Library of Australia

DEDICATION

First and foremost, *Kangaroo Stew* is dedicated to my fellow Tjupan/Ngalia Wonguktha people. The struggles, love and connection the characters in the text face are a pure reflection of my life and the lives of many Aboriginal and Torres Strait Islander peoples living in post-colonial society. This story is dedicated to all of my old people and to the old people of all of our mob that have had to bear the burden of desperately fighting to keep our culture and lore strong. Like our Tjukurr and songlines, your fights and tribulations will continue to live in our living memories, stories handed down from generation to generation of how we fought, we survived and eventually thrived once again.

I dedicate this text to all the lobbyists that spend their lives fighting for justice in a political landscape that empowers mining groups to destroy with reckless abandon. Your wisdom and foresight in keeping our parna (land) strong and healthy keep allyship meaningful and we walk hand in hand, protecting the needs of that which we hold so close.

Finally, I dedicate this story to my family, my children and to my dad, who has worked tirelessly in the mining space, doing the hardest work of creating change to the system from within the heart. Your wisdom and patience in the face of people that see no value in our landblood has helped construct an often balanced approach to the ways in which I can present stories such as *Kangaroo Stew.*

Nkayu kuturtu malya baal.

Love,
Zac Mongeeya James

CONTENTS

WRITER'S NOTES

Kangaroo Stew is based on a town named Leonora nestled on the edge of the desert. My Tjupan / Ngalia people were forced here in the 1970s after our traditional land was taken from us by various mining companies. The story is a representation of my experiences of Native Title, land rights and mining, which have changed, shifted and transformed through the stages of my life.

It is no secret that one of the greatest threats to our First Nations culture and lore is mining. The industry often destroys areas of great significance with little to no regard. This has been proven many times throughout the history of colonial Australia, with the explosion of Juukan Gorge being a recent example. That destruction is felt much deeper than just a scar on the parna (land). We feel that pain in our souls, our very beings. As a people of strong lore, the repercussions for destruction of songlines can be immense and draped in deep sorrow.

My people have long protested and fought against the mining industry, some notable activists in my family being Nan Shirley Wonyabong and my sister Vikki Abdulla. Their continued fight against uranium mining occurred in one of my sacred areas, Yakabindie. This is the birthplace of Jack, a character in the text.

There is opportunity in working with mining groups, opportunity that otherwise wouldn't exist for our forgotten communities in the remote areas. As my dad once said, 'It's better to have a seat at the table than watch our kids die in the streets'. Though this sentiment is valid and true, is it safe to make a deal with the devil? This conflict and inner turmoil between the importance of culture and land as well as future vision and sustainability in a post-colonial setting is the main conflict within *Kangaroo Stew*. It is a complex question which is the cause of great divide between many of my people. It is even a deep divide within myself as the writer.

My final thoughts are on the representation of strong, Blak matriarchal characters in text. For my people, our wanti (women) share equal balance in responsibilities in community. As men, we cherish their place as universe makers, mabarn (magic) healers, fierce protectors, wise oracles and fighters of justice and peace. Our women are superheroes but they grieve deep in the context of a colony that has strived to take everything from them and instilled a white patriarchal oppression upon them. The character of Lilly is a dedication to my mum, my nan, my aunties, my sister, my cousins, my daughter and all the change makers in the community who keep us strong. We would not exist without the universes that you create with great beauty and power, and we as Aboriginal men MUST fight to bring back sacred synchronicity; our songlines, culture and lore demand it.

DRAMATIS PERSONAE (CHARACTERS)

Lilly – Female, late 60s, Yamaji and Nyoongar. Mother of Jack and David. The Matriarch: strong, powerful and Blak.

John – Male, early 50s, Wonguktha, Martu, and a spirit. Father of Jack and David. A memory, living and eternal.

Jack – Male, early 30s, Wonguktha, Martu, Yamaji and Nyoongar. David's brother. Staunch and proud.

David – Male, late 20s, Wonguktha, Martu, Yamaji and Nyoongar. Jack's brother, Anne's fiance. Driven, loving but not always able to see the bigger picture.

Anne – Female, late 20s, Caucasian. David's fiancee.

TJUPANNY (LANGUAGE LIST)

Baal – (you)

Balu – Ba-loo (you)

Bana – (watch out, be careful)

Coord – (bro)

Dithi/Yalkana – (child)

Garlu Kata – (dickhead)

Gudi – (slang, crazy, tapped)

Gudyella – Ga-dee-ela (crazy, fool)

Inni – (true)

Kantula – Gan-jew-la (dance)

Kapi – Ga-bi (water)

Kata – (head)

Katja – Ga-cha (child)

Ladar – (warcry, shout)

Malya – (deadly, good)

Mama – Ma-ma (Dad)

Marlu – Ma-loo (Kangaroo)

Marnta – (ground, soil)

Mayi – (food)

Mirrinku – (death, died)

Moin – (sex, intercourse)

Munna – (arse, bum)

Murndah/Marnta – (dirt, money)

Nardoo – Nar-do (poxy)

Ninji – (spear)

Nintipayl – Nin-de-bi (knowledge)

Njayuku – Ni-u-goo (my)

Njobru – Nau-bru (girlfriend)

Njupa – (partner)

Nyaku – (goodbye, seeya)

Nyanji – (pubic hair)

Parna – Bar-nah (ground, earth)

Pika – Bee-gah (sick)

Pulya – (thank you, this is good)

Tjamu – (Pop, Grandfather)

Tjukurpa – Jewk-ar-ba (dreaming, culture)

Walyku – Wal-goo (poor thing, sad)

Wangka – One-gah (talk, speak)

Wati – (Loreman)

Wayunpa – Way-un-ba (welcome)

Wiardu – (nothing, no)

Winyarn – (poor thing)

Wirla – Whirl-a (heart)

Wongi – (us, our kind of people)

Wulanu – Wool-a-new (sad)

Yaku – Ya-goo (Mum)

Yukay – (watch out, bad thing)

Yuwa – You-wa (Yeh, hey? Hey!)

Creedence Clearwater Revival's 'Down on the Corner' plays.

SCENE ONE

KITCHEN

Song playing on the radio ('Up Around the Bend', CCR). LILLY *sits in contemplation at the kitchen table. She's drinking a tea as a pot boils on the stove. We see a calendar open on the table. She stands up, cuts some vegetables and puts them into the pot, then sits back down. Eventually she turns the calendar page over and stares at it. She turns it back over and gets back up and looks over the stew. She eyes a bottle of wine, then picks it up.*

JACK *(OS)* Door's jammed again.
(He is stuck behind the door.)

LILLY *places the bottle back down.*

LILLY You gotta kick it.

There's a banging sound.

ENTER JACK

JACK *is holding a bag of shopping.*

JACK I thought it was getting fixed today?
Smells good.

LILLY Have a taste.

JACK Where you want the shopping?

LILLY *motions to the fridge.* JACK *unpacks.*

LILLY Powder milk?

JACK Nothing, got condensed though.

LILLY What you mean 'got condensed'? Condensed milk? I'm not gonna use condensed milk on my Weeties!

JACK Oh I'm sorry Mum, I forgot you've got standards.

Powdered milk or nothing.

He pulls out a tin of powdered milk.

LILLY Make me wild some days.

JACK No-one else will put up with your high food standards.

LILLY Stop being cheeky.

JACK *finishes unpacking.*

JACK When's big shot due?

LILLY Don't start already. They hardly visit.

JACK Yuwa, why's he coming now? Asking for loan?

JACK *takes a seat, sees the wine bottle.*

JACK On the hooch again?

LILLY Funny. Like David would need a loan from us anyway.

JACK Maybe he lost his job?

LILLY Don't be stupid.

JACK *cracks a can and has a drink. He notices the calendar and flips over the pages.*

JACK You're a couple days behind there.

LILLY Really? I must have forgotten.

JACK Yeh right … 'Forgot'. I ran into Melanie at the shops.

LILLY What nuisance she been spreading?

JACK No nuisance, she said you've missed some sessions.

LILLY Wanted gossip most likely.

JACK She asked you to call for a coffee.

LILLY I will need wine for that.

JACK It might be good if you go talk to someone.

LILLY I'll go for that coffee the day you move to Perth.

JACK Ladar, low blow. I'm just looking out for ya.

LILLY Well go and look out for your brother.

JACK Ah yes, royalty approaches.

JACK *drinks the rest of his can and places it on the counter.*

JACK This isn't over.

JACK *goes to leave, but stops at the door. He turns back to say something but changes his mind.*

EXIT JACK

LILLY *sits in silence again. She stares at the calendar. She eventually stands and mixes the stew. She grabs the bottle and raises it to her lips but stops at the last minute. She puts down the bottle and places the calendar face down.*

SCENE TWO

FRONTYARD

ENTER ANNE *and* DAVID *with luggage.*

ANNE Relax, David.

DAVID I am relaxed.

ANNE If you're going to be this uptight the whole trip, just tell them already.

DAVID You know I can't do that.

ANNE Remember you're not just here for work.

DAVID How could I forget?

ANNE Stop. It. Now.

ANNE *gives* DAVID *a hug. He eventually hugs her back.*

ANNE Proper hug please.

DAVID You want me to use my legs or something?

ANNE Please.

DAVID *sighs and gives her a tighter hug, they relax into it.* DAVID'S *phone rings. He tries to answer but* ANNE *won't let him go.*

ANNE Nope.

DAVID I need to an—

ANNE Nope.

DAVID Anne …

He manages to get free, answering the phone.

DAVID *(To Anne)* Sorry ... *(To phone)* David speaking. Just got in now.

ANNE David, get off the phone.

DAVID *raises a hand.*

ANNE I'll hide your charger.

DAVID *(Phone)* Told you yesterday, we can't just ... No.

ENTER JACK

JACK *sees* DAVID *and* ANNE.

ANNE Jack!

JACK Anne.

They hug.

JACK How was the flight?

ANNE Pretty bumpy.

JACK And call centre?

ANNE He's been non-stop for the past week. Only time he's off the phone is when he shits.

JACK I'll steal his phone and hide it out in the backyard.

ANNE I'll get the charger, the rest is yours.

JACK Reckon he'd have a hissy fit?

ANNE His work would ... Wouldn't even give him time off for our visit.

JACK Inni? They know about Dad?

ANNE Yep.

DAVID *hangs up the phone.*

DAVID Jack!

DAVID *pulls* JACK *in for a hug,* JACK *is resistant.*

JACK I like the new earring.

DAVID Earring? I'm in the middle of negotiations, no rest—

DAVID'S *phone rings, he immediately answers it.*

JACK EXITS

DAVID And he's ... Gone. Two minutes in and already acting like an old man.

ANNE Maybe turn the phone off next time.

She kisses him on the cheek and leaves.

EXIT ANNE

DAVID *stands alone. Eventually he closes his eyes and breathes. He takes his shoes off and rubs his feet in the dirt. His phone rings and he immediately answers.*

EXIT DAVID

SCENE THREE

KITCHEN

ENTER LILLY

LILLY *is still mixing the stew. There's a commotion outside and the sound of a door getting whacked.*

ANNE		I think your door is broken.

LILLY		My goodness you looking prettier each time I see you.

ANNE		Right, just been travelling the whole day. Thanks though.

ENTER JACK

LILLY		Where David?

JACK		Business meeting.

ANNE		Work's got him on a tight leash.

LILLY		He needs to rest, that boy.

JACK		Don't we all.

LILLY		Nardoo sour puss.

JACK *makes his way to the fridge.*

JACK		What you want to drink Anne?

ANNE		Water or a juice is fine.

JACK		No juice but I can do you one better.

JACK *pulls out a carton of Black & Gold cordial.*

ANNE Nutritious and delicious.

JACK Only the best sis.

JACK *pours a glass and hands it to her.*

ANNE Is this stuff radioactive?

JACK Nah but you'll be seeing spirits in no time ...

LILLY Jack!

ANNE Thanks, I think?

JACK You right.

EXIT JACK

ANNE *looks around the kitchen.*

ANNE No dishwasher yet?

LILLY Wanted to put one in but I can't afford it.

ANNE We could help?

LILLY Wiardu, house is probably too old anyway.

There's a loud banging sound.

DAVID *(OS)* What the heck.

LILLY Door's jammed.

ANNE You gotta kick it.

ENTER DAVID

DAVID You should get that door fixed Mum.

LILLY I'm working on it.

LILLY *hugs* DAVID.

DAVID You good?

LILLY I'm doing alright. Now you going to tell me or what?

ANNE Good spot.

ANNE *lifts her hand and shows* LILLY *the engagement ring on her finger.*

ANNE David wanted to wait till we came back home.

DAVID We went on a little holiday and …

ANNE I was going to say no for a laugh.

LILLY It's beautiful! Did you help him choose?

ANNE No no, he picked it out himself. I had no idea it was even coming.

DAVID You sent me photos of rings every day.

ANNE Yeh … No idea at all.

LILLY You do know what good jewellery looks like hey?

DAVID Eyaa, that necklace we got for you was Jack's choice. I was gonna get you these butterfly earring things.

LILLY Glad you got the necklace then. That diamond is pretty big …

ANNE Well with David's promotion I think we could budget it in.

LILLY You got a promotion?

DAVID About five months ago.

LILLY Well … your dad would be proud.

DAVID I know he would Mum.

DAVID *walks to the pot and opens the lid.*

DAVID Chooo, Marlu?

LILLY Yuwa, but not ready yet.

ANNE I'll help set the table. You got the lug—

DAVID Already on it.

EXIT DAVID

ANNE *begins to set the table. A calm settles.*

ANNE How's work been?

LILLY Good, good. Biggest number of students attending this year.

ANNE Not surprised with the work you put in.

LILLY Seeing them kids all dressed up, big smiles, shining teeth … Always reminds me that no matter what, them little shit bags make it worth it in the end.

Table continues to be set. LILLY *goes back to the stew.*

ANNE The town looks different this time of year.

LILLY Rains freshen the place up. Nothing better than seeing that bright green shining on red dirt.

ENTER JACK

JACK Smelling good.

LILLY *serves the stew up and the three sit.*

LILLY DINNER'S READY!

DAVID *(OS)* Coming!

They eat.

ANNE I still remember the first time I tried roo stew.

JACK 'No you can't eat Skippy.'

ANNE I'd never eaten roo before then.

LILLY David was that excited to bring you home. Set the table and everything.

ANNE He gave me fifty lessons in 'cultural protocols' before we got here … Worried I'd be scared by you two.

JACK I was gonna do a smoking ceremony when you arrived and make you skin a goanna.

LILLY Jack!

JACK Mucking 'round sis! Just the goanna …

ENTER DAVID

DAVID *sits down, rubbing his hands together. He digs in.*

DAVID So brus, you still got that woman you were shacked up with before?

JACK Fiona.

DAVID Yeh Fiona. How you two?

JACK We broke up.

DAVID Nardoo. Wasn't she a reiki healer or something?

JACK Naturopath. I think … She made me drink lots of weird shit, made me do a lot of weird shits.

DAVID Aye I thought she was gonna start playing didje …

JACK Oi.

DAVID Gammon brus!

JACK Nah you right, she wasn't the right one.

Awkward scraping of cutlery. ANNE *elbows* DAVID.

DAVID Anne and I are thinking of going out to see Dad's grave on Friday if you want to come.

JACK Maybe, I'll let you know.

DAVID Yep cool. Cool, cool, coooool.

Silence.

LILLY Have you two thought of a date yet?

ANNE We were thinking spring next year.

JACK You two going for another holiday?

LILLY Didn't they tell you Jack?

JACK Tell me what?

DAVID We getting married.

JACK True god?

ANNE Seriously!

LILLY Deadly hey?

JACK True! Malya for you both! When were you gonna tell me ya big gudyella?

DAVID I thought we could go for a beer later, was gonna have a yarn then.

JACK Gohn then! The little brother getting married. Your shout though hey?

DAVID I got ya.

DAVID'S *phone rings.*

DAVID Shit.

ANNE *snatches the phone and stands, holding it away from* DAVID.

ANNE It's Friday night. Just let it ring out David.

DAVID Anne you know I need to get this.

ANNE Tell them to give you a break Davie.
It's bloody enough!

DAVID ANNE! *(Answers)* David speaking …

EXIT DAVID, ANNE FOLLOWS

Silence.

JACK *scoops* DAVID'S *leftovers into his own bowl.*

JACK Can't believe they're getting married.

LILLY Cry me a river.

JACK Surprised he has time for someone else.

LILLY Go talk with your brother instead of sooking.

JACK I want to but … I think I need to book in advance.

ENTER ANNE

LILLY You right?

ANNE Um … Yeh just feeling a bit crook. Thanks for dinner but I think I'll go to bed.

LILLY Is he on phone still?

ANNE *nods.*

ANNE Think I'll get ready for sleep, been a long day.

EXIT ANNE

ENTER DAVID

DAVID Where's Anne?

LILLY Gone to bed I think.

DAVID And where's my stew?

JACK Thought you weren't coming back.

DAVID Greedy frick. Always stealing my feed.

JACK *scoops bare scraps back into* DAVID'S *bowl.*

DAVID Yeh, thanks.

He eats.

LILLY David …

DAVID What?

LILLY You said hello yet?

DAVID Not yet.

JACK You even remember how to?

DAVID Piss off Jack. I'll do it when I can.

LILLY Why do you have to be like that?

JACK I'm just asking.

EXIT JACK

LILLY I'm glad you're back Davie.

DAVID Me too.

LILLY Have you told Anne?

DAVID About Dad?

Shakes his head.

LILLY Well you better do it quick.

DAVID Yeh. I should've done it a while ago.

LILLY You not going to have a choice now.

DAVID I know. I'm going to bed.

LILLY Sleep tight.

DAVID Night Mum.

EXIT DAVID

LILLY *sits at the table and looks at the calendar. She lifts it up and flips the pages to the right date. She stares at it for a while.*

ENTER JOHN

JOHN *sits at the table.*

JOHN Getting married hey.

LILLY John.

She grabs the bottle of red and loosens the cap. She raises it to her lips but stops herself from drinking. She places the bottle on the table and exits. JOHN *is left alone.*

SCENE FOUR

BEDROOM

ENTER ANNE, DAVID

ANNE *fumes while unpacking clothes, occasionally throwing daggers to a totally oblivious* DAVID.

ANNE I can't believe you took that phone call.

DAVID I had to! I'm just trying to work out these bloody site specifics.

ANNE *staggers to bed,* DAVID *runs to her.*

DAVID ANNE!

David picks her up.

DAVID Hey, hey, hey! What's happening?

ANNE My stomach's killing me.

DAVID *helps* ANNE *onto the bed.*

DAVID You feel sick?

ANNE No, just pain …

DAVID I'll get your waterbottle, you stay in bed.

ANNE *lays down,* DAVID *gets her water then waterbottle.*

ANNE Turn the lights off, they're hurting my eyes.

DAVID *turns the lights off.*

DAVID Better?

ANNE *grunts in response.*

SCENE FIVE

KITCHEN

LILLY *is on her phone. A photo is next to her on the table. She puts her phone down, and a man stands in the corner of the room, in the darkness. It is* JOHN.

LILLY All the books say that time makes wounds fade, well they're all fucking liars cause it's been sixteen years. The days fly off the calendar and I keep thinking, if time is real, why can't I just forget? The closer it gets to the day, the more I see your stupid, beautiful smile in my eyelids. I still smell you; leather jacket, petrol and rain on dust. I can even remember the way your lips would taste of red wine when we kissed. Every time I see the day drawing closer, a movie plays in my head. Except it's not a movie, it's a loop. I get trapped in this loop, this pocket of memory I can't escape from. I can see you, living, breathing. Is sixteen years not penance enough?

LILLY *throws the photo in the corner, it shatters. She grabs the bottle of red, unscrews it and drinks deep.* JOHN *walks behind her, attempts to place a hand on her shoulder but stops himself.*

EXIT JOHN

SCENE SIX

BEDROOM

DAVID *and* ANNE *are asleep.*

ENTER JOHN

JOHN *sits on the edge of the bed. He sets a spear on the ground and looks into the distance.*

JOHN I know why you're here.

DAVID *stirs in his sleep.*

JOHN The ground still feels your blood my son.

DAVID What ... What's going on?

JOHN *tickles* DAVID'S *feet then laughs.*

DAVID Dad?

JOHN Evening young fella.

Silence.

JOHN No hello?

DAVID This isn't the right time.

JOHN Cause your woman lying there?

DAVID Yes cause my woman's laying there!

JOHN You gonna introduce me or what?

DAVID What? Why are you here? I haven't heard from you in years.

JOHN You haven't been back home in years.

DAVID Yeh I have—

JOHN Not at the right time.

DAVID Look … Can we do this another time?

JOHN David, you need my help now.

ANNE *moves in her sleep.*

DAVID Fuck. Dad, go away. I don't have time for your spirit guide bullshit!

JOHN Aye katja, njayuku nintipayl wangka balu.

You and your njupa are in danger!

ANNE David?

DAVID GET OUT OF HERE!

JOHN EXITS

ANNE David, why the hell are you screaming?!

DAVID I had a bad dream.

ANNE You're bloody drenched!

DAVID *gets out of bed.*

DAVID I'm going to have a shower …

ANNE Yeh. Can you pass me my water?

DAVID Kapi …

EXIT DAVID

SCENE SEVEN

KITCHEN

LILLY *is sitting at the table with her head down. The bottle of red is on its side. The photo frame lies shattered on the floor.*

DAVID *(OS)* Hey Mum, you still awake?

LILLY *wakes up with a shock and hides the wine.*

ENTER DAVID

DAVID Shit, what happened?

LILLY Nothing, just dropped a photo is all.

DAVID Bana, you dropped it off a building. Pulya? You ok? You look ... Horrors. Are you bloody drinking again? I thought you were getting better.

LILLY What do you mean better?

DAVID Nothing.

Silence.

DAVID Dad was in my room.

LILLY What happened?

DAVID He was warning me.

LILLY About what?

DAVID I don't know.

Silence.

LILLY You need to start listening to your spirits. If he comes back to you again, pay attention.

DAVID I will, I just, don't know … What if she leaves?

LILLY Anne? Why would she ever leave?

DAVID Ah, dunno Mum. Maybe cause the ghost of my dad is walking around the poxy house!

LILLY David. You are a black man. We are a black family. This is the way it is.

DAVID What, all black fellas have a ghost in their house?

LILLY Don't be stupid. Just the Wongi ones. Look I'm going to sleep, turn the lights off when you go to bed.

DAVID Yuwa.

EXIT LILLY

DAVID *looks at the photo and the bottle of wine.*

EXIT DAVID

SCENE EIGHT

FRONTYARD

The next morning.

ENTER JOHN

The sun rises, we can hear butcher birds singing in the distance. JOHN *stands and looks over the yard.*

ENTER JACK

JACK *walks in with a cup of tea, he sees* JOHN.

JACK Yuwa mama!

JOHN Wayunpa katja.

They hug.

JACK Balu wangka, yaku?

JOHN Yuwa … Walyku, walyku …

JACK Yaku pika wirla, nardoo.

JOHN Yuwa. Njayuku wirla wulanu balu.

They stand in silence.

JACK Davie's home.

JOHN I know, seen him already.

JACK Aye? You see Anne?

JOHN His njupa? She pika.

JACK Sick?

JOHN Yuwa. Talk to him.

JACK I'm trying. He's being a big shot though.

JOHN Jack. He's not himself.

JACK Yuwa.

JOHN *looks for a while longer then walks away.*

EXIT JOHN

JACK *puts his cuppa down and picks up his hurt, old football.*

ENTER DAVID

DAVID *is holding a cup of coffee.*

DAVID Always playing with the footy aye big ole.

JACK It's better than having a phone glued to my head.

DAVID *drinks, there's an uncomfortable silence.*

DAVID There any good cafés here yet?

JACK Nescafe not good enough for your Melbourne tastebuds?

DAVID Just cause we black doesn't mean we need to drink dirt water.

JACK That 'dirt water' coffee costs around $60 a tin out near Wiluna.

DAVID I saw that. Disgrace unna. Ripping mob off like that.

JACK That's the way it goes out that way. Whiteballa create the terms, the conditions, the prices and the law.

DAVID Nardoo. So … There's not a café?

JACK BP has a new machine. Sure you could humbug them for something quality, they your brother boys hey.

DAVID Shut your dot.

JACK Mucking round. Condensed milk there.

JACK *kicks the footy.*

DAVID Condensed milk … I'd rather drink dirt water.

DAVID'S *phone buzzes. He puts it away.*

DAVID Give us a kick.

JACK Don't kick it over the fence.

DAVID I was a little kid last time!

JACK You still got little kid legs now.

They kick.

JACK Kick straight, otherwise you're doing the dance.

DAVID Which one?

JACK How'd it go again?

JACK *shakes a leg and dances, it's winyarn.*

JACK I'm a Barbie girl, in a Barbie world.

DAVID Come on now. At least do it right.

DAVID *shakes a leg and dances, it's somehow worse.*

DAVID I'm blue dabu deba, da dab de!

JACK That's him! Haven't seen that one for a while. You used to think you were so deadly too. Remember that disco the cops ran at the old gym?

DAVID Choo, 'Wipeout' on repeat all night.

They both do a dance to 'Wipeout'.

JACK You been practising your moves?

DAVID It is a well-established fact that Wongis cannot dance.

JACK Nah brus, Dad just said that to make you feel better.

They kick.

DAVID Wasn't that the first time you and Fiona went for moin?

JACK Aye … You wouldn't leave us alone the whole night.

DAVID I was trying to hang out with my bro. I'm sorry to hear she's gone.

JACK Yeh. Yeh that was a shock.

DAVID Probably not for her.

JACK What you mean?

DAVID Couldn't she read the future or something?

JACK Gudi ways. She'd look at tea leaves and start crying every morning. If you say something gonna happen every day, eventually it'll happen.

DAVID You alright?

JACK Yuwa. Thinking of going down Perth for a little while, spread my wings a little.

DAVID That what you call it these days hey?

BEAT

DAVID Can't believe this old thing still got air in it. Probably have better luck kicking a rat.

JACK You're meant to kick with your feet not your shins. What them watjelas been teaching you over there?

DAVID Calm down Franklin.

JACK It's Micky Walters, get it right. Good being home?

DAVID It's been good. Good to smell the air, feel the grass.

JACK You mean dirt?

DAVID Yuwa. It's good to see Mum again. You as well ya grumpy dawg.

JACK You seen Dad?

DAVID *shrugs.*

JACK What's that mean?

DAVID I don't know bro, just leave it hey?

JACK Does Anne know he's here?

DAVID No.

JACK Why haven't you told her?

DAVID We're getting married soon, I'll tell her then.

JACK You been married up for long time already.

DAVID Yeh but …

JACK Your choice. I don't know why you wouldn't tell her but … Don't know why you do a lot of things.

DAVID C'mon now.

JACK Messing with you. Despite your many, many shortcomings, I'm happy for you two.

They sit, DAVID'S *phone buzzes again.*

JACK Anne said you were here for work.

DAVID There's an area up north way we want to have a look at. Here to sign papers—

JACK David, that's our parna …

DAVID Nah, nah bro, don't worry. I'm just here to check it out.

JACK You're gonna say no right?

DAVID *ponders.*

DAVID I dunno brus …

JACK You dunno … There's no way you could go ahead with it. What about Elder mob? You can't ignore them.

DAVID I haven't made any choices yet. Look, this deal could be worth billions Jack, I'm talking a lot of royalty money for us as well. We could get Mum out of here, back in a flash house. You could go and live in Perth!

JACK Don't be dumb, this our land, our parna. This is our Tjukurpa!

DAVID Fuck's sake Jack. You gonna be a responsible fucking adult or what?

JACK Watch it, Jacinta Price.

DAVID I love this country as much as you—

JACK Do you?

DAVID It just comes to a point where you need to come back to society.

JACK Society? You mean chucking drills in the ground and digging up our ancestors?

DAVID You deserve more than this. Mum deserves more than this! The house is falling apart, the backyard's trashed and this place fucking stinks.

JACK You forgot to mention the coffee. You know what? Fuck ya. Not even worth it.

JACK *moves to exit.*

DAVID Wait.

JACK Why?

DAVID Cause we need to talk. Whatever this shit is, we gotta work it out.

JACK *stops.*

JACK Well talk then.

DAVID I know it's been hard since Dad died but—

DAVID *is cut off by the sound of his phone ringing. There is a beat before he checks who is calling.*

DAVID Shit.

JACK Guess you should get that hey?

EXIT JACK

DAVID Jack! Ah fuck! *(Answering)* Yes hello, this is David speaking.

EXIT DAVID

SCENE NINE

KITCHEN

ANNE *and* LILLY *sit at the dinner table. They're both looking a bit shabby.*

ANNE I don't know, I finished dinner, headed to bed and then got hit with this sickness. Thought it might've been the stew but I haven't thrown up. I'm still feeling shocking now.

LILLY Cuppa tea might fix you up love.

LILLY *gets up to prepare tea. She struggles.*

ANNE Don't worry, I'll get it.

ANNE *prepares the tea.*

ANNE Don't take this the wrong way, but you look like you had a rough night too.

LILLY No offence taken.

ANNE How long's it been since you quit drinking?

LILLY Ten months.

ANNE *sees the calendar.*

ANNE It's his anniversary soon hey. David's dad.

LILLY On Friday.

ANNE I know it's been a long time, but you can talk with me if you need.

LILLY That's not your burden to carry.

ANNE I'm part of this family.

LILLY I've got work to keep me steady.

ANNE Lil—

LILLY *brushes her off.*

LILLY How far along are you?

ANNE What?

LILLY How far along are you?

ANNE What do you mean?

LILLY Baby girl, one thing I've inherited from my nan is an eye and a nose for things left unspoken.

ANNE Three months, give or take a few days, but …

LILLY *gives* ANNE *a hug.*

LILLY Does David know?

ANNE Of course.

LILLY So that's why he's working so hard.

ANNE I keep telling him we'll be ok but he won't relax.

LILLY That's just his way of dealing with things.

ANNE Well I guess I'll have to warn David it's not a secret anymore.

LILLY Ok love.

EXIT LILLY – ENTER DAVID

LILLY *laughs as she walks past* DAVID.

LILLY See youuuu.

DAVID I stuffed up.

ANNE How?

DAVID With Jack. Baldwin has been on my back calling non-stop and … I don't know what to do. I feel like a sellout. I'm doing it for the family though, right? I keep telling myself that. Maybe I'm just doing it for the pay cheque. Fuck.

ANNE Look, I know this is a hard moment but you're trying to do what's best, for everyone.

DAVID Yeh …

ANNE I know your family will support you.

DAVID Not if I sell our entire identity for fuck all.

ANNE It's not fuck all. It's stability, sustainability, community strength. You know it's the right thing!

DAVID This isn't the same as them other mob.

ANNE Why? Why can't your family be secure?

DAVID Cause … It's different.

ANNE Well … If it helps, we don't need to tell your mum anymore.

DAVID You told her about the mine?

ANNE What? No …

She points to her belly.

DAVID Thank fuck …

DAVID *readjusts.*

DAVID Was she … happy?

ANNE *nods.* DAVID *pulls her into a hug.*

DAVID Come here.

They kiss, then stand in silence, holding each other.

ANNE It's going to be ok.

DAVID What is?

ANNE Jack. Work. It'll be ok.

DAVID Yuwa.

Colours slowly begin to fade and a gentle fog drifts in. It is dark with an orange tinge, almost twilight. Wind echoes.

DAVID I need to tell you something. Anne?

DAVID *lets go of* ANNE.

ANNE EXITS

DAVID Anne? Anne?!

ENTER JOHN

DAVID God dammit. Dad?

JOHN *motions for* DAVID *to follow.*

JOHN It's time.

DAVID Time for what?

JOHN We need to go now.

DAVID Dammit! Wait for me.

SCENE TEN

IN THE TJUKURPA

ENTER JOHN *and* DAVID

JOHN *picks up two spears and a shield.*

DAVID Dad what's going on, what is this place?

JOHN Take this spear, ninji.

JOHN *gives* DAVID *a spear and the shield.*

DAVID Where are we?

JOHN I'll tell you later.

DAVID Old man, you better tell me right now.

JOHN Katja, you're in danger. I need you to trust me.

DAVID Maybe I've been working too much.

JOHN Davie.

DAVID I'm having a mental breakdown or something.

JOHN Davie, this is real.

DAVID I should have just turned my phone off.

There's a shriek in the distance.

JOHN Katja, be quiet. If you're dreaming or not, there's danger here. I need you to follow.

JOHN *walks. The two reach a point.* DAVID *sits, and* JOHN *hands a spear to him. A shadow stands behind* DAVID, *and it shrieks.*

JOHN This is the place in between. It floats within the physical reality you perceive. A place of life, of the earth and the Tjukurpa. There is no light without dark and those creatures live from the darkness. Just after the creation of our worlds, when life was just beginning, there was only the Spirit of creation. Spirit shaped the animals and trees and gave them oxygen from its own mouth. Spirit lived for its creations and loved them all for they were an extension of itself.

After an eternity of watching its creations live and love, Spirit became lonely and so, it split an image of itself into existence. This was Shadow. Though there was great peace and harmony between the two, Shadow intervened with the creatures it watched over. Spirit asked Shadow to withdraw, Shadow refused. See, while Spirit had split itself to create Shadow, it had not granted the power of life and this made Shadow jealous. They began to fight.

JOHN *starts the Spirt and Shadow dance.*

JOHN The war was long and many lives were lost. Spirit captured Shadow and banished it to the earth, cursing it with mortality. Once Shadow reached the Earth's land, it crumbled into a human. The first human. Knowing how much misery loneliness can create, Spirit crafted another being to join Shadow, her name was

Parna. From then, humanity grew to what it is now.

JOHN *finishes his story.*

JOHN That place you want to dig? It's where Spirit landed.

DAVID I'm not digging anything …

JOHN It's sacred area, special site David. Mirrinku.

EXIT JOHN

Natural lighting returns. DAVID *looks out in the distance, tries to imitate how John danced.*

ENTER ANNE

ANNE *is dazed.*

ANNE David? Where are you?

DAVID Anne?

DAVID *can't see her, he continues dancing and then turns to see her watching him.*

ANNE Wha—

DAVID Just dancing …

ANNE Why?

DAVID It's a long story.

ANNE Ok crazy, where'd you go?

DAVID I dunno.

ANNE What do ya mean?

Silence.

DAVID Baby … Culture things. I don't know how to explain it. If I could I would.

ANNE Can't you try?

DAVID I said I don't know how!

ANNE Fine. Whatever. Don't have to be a dickhead about it.

ANNE *walks inside,* DAVID *follows.*

DAVID Where are ya going?

ANNE Bed. I need a nap.

EXIT DAVID *and* ANNE

SCENE ELEVEN

KITCHEN

LILLY *sits next to the phone, somehow it's still a cable phone. She's trying to end her conversation.*

LILLY Yeh look Melanie, I need to go. What's that? Sleeping with who? Can't be talking that way! C'mon now, how would you even know if that's true? Well if it's on Facebook I better believe ya then! I was being facetious. God in heaven, let them be then. We don't need a protest. We don't need a protest! You making me wild! What's that now? For heaven's sake I already told Jodi I don't need the job, like a broken record. I gotta go, dinner is almost—

ENTER YOUNG JOHN

YOUNG JOHN *sits at the table. He is wearing different clothes.*

Y/JOHN Cuppa please Lil.

LILLY What? No, no I'm here still. What about June's dog? Son, I meant son.

Y/JOHN Cheers.

YOUNG JOHN *takes an invisible cup of tea and drinks it.*

Y/JOHN I've had a yarn to the Elders, they said no.

LILLY I have to go.

She hangs up the phone.

LILLY John?

Y/JOHN What'd you expect Lil? This was never going to be easy.

LILLY What are you doing?

YOUNG JOHN *pauses and looks in the distance.*

Y/JOHN That I'll die? I'll get sick? It's not real!

LILLY Stuck in a loop …

She slowly reaches out but then stops. A bottle of red is on the table.

Y/JOHN To keep all our mob alive and not dying on the street!

LILLY *grabs the bottle and sculls from it.*

EXIT LILLY *and* YOUNG JOHN

SCENE TWELVE

KITCHEN

DAVID *is on the phone.*

DAVID Yeh look, I think we need more time …

ENTER JACK

DAVID I haven't been out there yet. Because my fiancee has been sick as a dog and I'm trying to see my family. Yes. Sorry Mr Baldwin. Yes. I'll let you know. Ok. Ok.

DAVID *sighs and hangs up his phone. The two eye each other,* DAVID *softens his resolve.*

DAVID Anne's a bit better.

JACK Might be the pregnancy?

DAVID You know?

JACK Yuwa, knew when I first saw her. And Mum told me.

DAVID Course she did. Might be the pregnancy but I'm not sure …

JACK What's up?

DAVID Something weird has been going on.

JACK Let me guess, you've been seeing Dad?

DAVID Don't worry.

JACK Stop talking shit.

DAVID Jack, I want to talk to you, but I can't.

JACK Ahh you garlu kata! If you're gonna speak in riddles, keep your hole shut.

DAVID Frick.

JACK Why you acting like Dad's not here? He's been coming back the same time for sixteen years. You used to get excited and now you're pretending it's not even happening.

DAVID Yeh, I was a kid and you just kept encouraging me instead of helping me grieve my dad dying—

JACK Bull shit. You've just been cutting away your connection to country. Hmm? Baal parna wiardu? That's why you're here, to dig it up inni?

DAVID My job doesn't make me a bad person. I'm trying to do this for us.

JACK Fuck off, there's no us. There's just you. You, you, you. That's why ya ran off to Perth as soon as you could hey?

DAVID It wasn't like that.

JACK Yeh, fuck around in Perth. Lose your colour, lose your spirit.

DAVID Aye …

JACK That's why you just up and left Mum behind. Left her with nothing.

DAVID I was nineteen! Mum shouldn't have been our burden.

JACK Then what about our land? Our dreaming?

DAVID They're gonna dig everything up no matter what ya dumb frick! Section 18 is the only real law in this land.

JACK Well you better tell that to your kid when their Tjukurpa is gone! Lost cause our home has been raped for diamonds and dishwashers.

DAVID Dreaming doesn't pay for electricity!

JACK How would you know? You've never spent a minute living it!

BEAT

JACK Decided about the mine site then?

DAVID Shut ya hole.

JACK Just imagine rolling around in all them mountains of green. Shoving it up your munna and wherever else you put it.

DAVID Ladar Jack. Stop now—

JACK You know what? You're about the most opposite of Dad that there can be. Dad told us we gotta care about the land, to grow it, nurture it! What do you think he'd be thinking if he saw you? Selling yourself for a handful of diamonds!

DAVID Dad's dead! He's dead and you don't know what he's thinking so shut the hell up!

JACK Don't talk about him like that, you fucking coconut.

DAVID *lunges at* JACK, *they shirtfront each other and then push away, shaping up and circling each other.* DAVID *gets a few jabs in but* JACK *lands an uppercut and drops* DAVID *to the floor. He lays into him.*

ENTER ANNE

ANNE Hey! Stop it you two!

ANNE *tries to stop them but is ignored, her belly begins to fill with pain.*

JACK You chose to come back here on the date our dad died and rip up our land. You ain't my fucking brother.

DAVID Don't walk around like you're some culture boss. Just cause you decided to waste your life instead of doing something with it.

JACK You don't even know what Tjukurpa is. Fucking watjela.

DAVID What you call me?

ANNE *drops to the ground, groaning.*

JACK A. Fucking. Watjela.

They shirtfront again, they fight and end up wrestling on the ground.

ENTER LILLY

LILLY *is holding a bottle of red, she is obviously drunk.*

LILLY Hey what's going on. Anne?

She checks ANNE.

LILLY ANNE'S NOT BREATHING!

DAVID What? ANNE!

JACK FUCK! See what you done!

DAVID Anne? Anne wake up. Anne.

JACK You making everyone sick you fu—

DAVID Call an ambulance NOW.

LILLY What'd you do?

JACK *(Talking into phone)* Yeh, corner of Charles Street, please get here quick, she's pregnant.

DAVID I DON'T KNOW!

JACK PLEASE HURRY!

DAVID ANNE!

LIGHTS FADE

SCENE THIRTEEN

BEDROOM/KITCHEN

Stage dark

ANNE *lies on her bed,* DAVID *sleeps on a chair next to it.* LILLY *is sitting at the kitchen table.*

ENTER JACK

JACK *walks into the kitchen with two coffees.*

JACK Shouldn't you be at the pub?

LILLY Ah, give it a rest.

Walks into DAVID *and* ANNE'S *room.*

JACK David.

He places the coffees down and taps DAVID, *no response.*

JACK David? I brought some coffee, from BP.

DAVID *shuffles but stays asleep.* JACK *places a hand on his shoulder, comforting.* JACK *walks back into the loungeroom.*

LILLY Nurse said her condition is stable …

JACK Bubba still hasn't gotten any better.

LILLY Hormone levels are ok though.

JACK Whatever that means.

LILLY Heart rate is just a bit low.

Silence.

LILLY What the hell were you thinking? Because of you two and your immature bullshit … She might lose bub.

JACK It was an accident.

LILLY Thank god for that! What were you fighting about? David's only been in town for a couple nights.

JACK Don't get high and mighty on me. On the grog again. How long has that been going for?

LILLY Jack.

JACK Shit, I don't care anymore Mum.

BEAT

JACK Did he tell you why he's here?

LILLY For the anniversary.

JACK The first time in ten years? Didn't you wonder why he's always on the phone?

LILLY He says he's working.

JACK And what does he do? Mining.

LILLY So?

JACK He's here to approve a dig site out near the ranges. That's why we've been fighting!

LILLY No …

DAVID'S *phone rings.*

LILLY Baldwin?

JACK Mean something?

LILLY It used to.

JACK Mum?

LILLY *leaves the room and* JACK *follows, stopping and looking back, then continuing out the door. As* JACK *leaves, colours shift to the alternate world, dark green and blue.* DAVID *slowly wakes up.*

DAVID Dad?

The scene changes. He walks through the kitchen.

DAVID Dad?

SCENE FOURTEEN

FRONTYARD

JOHN *stands looking into the distance.*

DAVID Did you do this to her?

JOHN *is silent, doesn't know what to say.*

DAVID Dad? Did you?

JOHN I made a mistake.

DAVID What have you done?

JOHN Not with Anne, with you. There are things you need to know. Tjukurpa, parna. When I died, I took them with me.

DAVID What are some stories about land gonna help with—

JOHN LISTEN. This parna isn't something to be mined. Our culture doesn't come from gold and diamonds, it comes from our Tjukurpa. From our family, our history. If you forget, the family forgets. You forget Tjukurpa, you forget parna, then our Tjukurpa is lost. You think it don't matter but it does katja.

DAVID What has this got to do with Anne?

JOHN It has everything to do with her!

DAVID How?!

JOHN Mining parna is killing our Tjukurpa!

DAVID Fuck. What do you want me to do Dad? What the hell am I meant to do? Our young fellas are killing themselves out there cause they've got nothing. Our home got more mental health problems than most the world. Have a look on the street there! Aunties living in third world conditions. Kids running round with nothing, sixty bucks for a pack of chops at the shops. Old people don't even have murndah for bullets and petrol to go shoot a marlu. We got no money, we got no houses and you want me to sit here and turn down the one option we might have to survive this. I can't Dad. You just don't see it. You don't wanna see it.

There's nothing left we can do. We have no power here, they took it all. What, you want me to jump on the media and make a petition to stop the government? It's the government Dad. They are choosing to do this to us, to our people. They are choosing to kill us, destroy us. What, we gonna round up all the 303s and sit up on the hills and shoot them miners when they come to dig? We'll get massacred, again. We're not gonna get justice for what's happened before, we won't even get justice for what's happening now! Just ... Look around the world. Nobody gives a fuck about our culture. Nobody. It's only us and if we don't do something, there won't even be an us to save anymore.

JOHN And who are you to make these decisions katja? You not even a Wati, you dithi.

DAVID I am a man.

JOHN Not our way. Not proper way. You can't come here and make these decisions.

DAVID What are they going to do if I don't?

JOHN You'll die, Davie!

DAVID *scoffs.*

JOHN If you not listening, I'll show you.

JOHN *places a hand on* DAVID'S *head. The stage blacks out.*

1997

DAVID *is back in 1997. Lights come up and he is standing in the centre of the living room.*

ENTER LILLY *and* JOHN *dressed in 90s attire*

LILLY *walks through the front door.* JOHN *carries a bag with a roo tail in it.*

DAVID Mum?

LILLY You right with them tails?

JOHN Yeh I got 'em.

JOHN *and* LILLY *unpack their things,* JOHN *places the tail on the table.* DAVID *walks between the two, waving his hands in front of their faces, no response. An answering machine light blinks near a phone,* LILLY *plays it.*

LEO V/O John, it's Leo.

LILLY John, get here quick.

JOHN What?

LEO V/O Look. I've talked to them again and the answer is still no. The Elders and Wati all said no. I'm sorry.

Answering machine ends and there's silence. JOHN *replays the message.*

LEO V/O John, it's Leo. Look. I've talked to them again and the answer is still no. The Elders and Wati all said no. I'm—

JOHN Fuck!

Silence.

LILLY So that's it then?

JOHN No. Baldwin is on my back to get signatures. If Aunty Yas and Leo can't convince Pop to say yes, the dig will initiate without our blessing. Without our cut.

DAVID Baldwin?

JOHN *takes a seat, head in his hands.* LILLY *sits next to him.* DAVID *stands next to them.*

LILLY Look I know the extra money will be good but maybe …

JOHN We can't afford to turn it down.

LILLY What'd you expect?

JOHN A conversation. I don't think Aunty May knows we need the money.

LILLY Just remember you don't speak for the whole family.

JOHN The hell does that mean?

LILLY You're not responsible for everyone.

JOHN Everyone? This could set US up—

LILLY It's about more than money!

JOHN *stands.*

JOHN I know how it works. Don't try lecture me about my own people.

EXIT JOHN *and* LILLY

DAVID *sits at the table, alone in the room, the phone rings again, answering machine takes the message.*

LEO V/O You're gonna die if you don't stop this, John. This isn't just your country. You can't be the only one to speak for it. Stop being gudyella. Our spirit is in that parna, our Tjukurpa is all through there. Watjelas have already taken so much from us, do not let them take more.

DAVID Like father, like son.

Lights shift.

ENTER LILLY *and* JOHN

LILLY Stop!

JOHN Out of my way.

LILLY Why are you doing this?

JOHN Piss off.

JOHN *walks outside and slams the door shut.*

EXIT JOHN

LILLY *sits at the table, head in her hands.*

DAVID I remember this, that's the day you died …

Lights fade.

PRESENT DAY

JOHN *takes his hand off* DAVID'S *head.*

JOHN You can't let them dig Davie. You can't.

EXIT JOHN

EXIT DAVID

SCENE FIFTEEN

KITCHEN

ENTER LILLY

LILLY *runs into the kitchen. She starts scrambling with a pot and ingredients, hastily chopping up vegetables and adding them into the pot.*

ENTER JACK

JACK What are you doing? What's happening right now?

LILLY *grabs a bottle of wine and sculls from it.*

JACK Aye!

JACK *tries to wrestle the bottle from her, she refuses, holding tight.*

JACK Stop Mum.

LILLY No.

JACK Give me the bo—

LILLY LET IT GO NOW.

JACK *lets go, stepping back.* LILLY *sculls and sculls until the bottle is empty. She drops it to the ground. She finishes the next bottle. Desperate, she finds her cooking bottle and sculls it. The kangaroo stew is burning.*

LILLY He always leaves when I drink. I've wasted my whole life in this stupid shit hole of a town with nothing to show for it! I'm sick of being stuck in this place. I want to be free, I want to travel the seas but I'm stuck here. Even this grog doesn't help anymore. I can't tell if I'm sleepwalking or just asleep. I drink cause it's the only thing that makes your dad go away.

JACK I thought you wanted him here.

LILLY You think I like being trapped in love? You think I want to be lost in memories. He's torturing me!

JACK Don't say that—

LILLY If I don't get rid of him, Davie's going to die.

JACK I think you should lie down ...

JACK *helps* LILLY *make her way to her bed.*

LILLY You know why your dad died. Don't let your brother do the same.

EXIT JACK *and* LILLY

There's silence on stage except for the sound of a bubbling stew.

ENTER DAVID

DAVID *sees the stew and runs to mix it.*

ENTER JACK

DAVID Stew's stuffed.

JACK Mum's sick, Anne's sick and I know you know why.

DAVID What?

JACK Enough of the bullshit. It's time you listen to Dad and do what you have to.

DAVID I need a minute brus.

JACK You don't have a minute.

DAVID I already asked what I need to do, he doesn't know.

JACK Alright.

JACK *starts the spirit dance.*

DAVID What you doing?

JACK You know the dance, join.

DAVID C'mon bro—

JACK Join.

JOHN *enters unbeknownst to the brothers. Tapping his sticks, the boys slowly fall into synchronicity,* JOHN *mirroring the moves behind the two. The lights flick between reality and the dreamscape. Eventually they completely shift. The three sit in the space. The lights flash back to reality.*

JOHN So what's the plan, Davie?

Silence.

DAVID I'm going to tell Baldwin the deal's off.

JACK *smiles.*

DAVID That's only a bandaid though.

JACK It's a start.

DAVID It's a start. Those companies are still coming. You know if it's not Baldwin, it'll be some other person.

JOHN Then you gotta think a different way, don't you?

DAVID Yuwa. Protect what we can.

JACK Nah coord, we at a new chapter now. We don't have to get the scraps anymore, we got a seat at the table.

DAVID One step at a time.

DAVID *stands and looks over the backyard. He reaches down and grabs a handful of red dirt. He shifts it through his hands then lets it drop.*

JACK What happens after David makes the call?

JOHN I go. I move on.

JACK You gonna be gone for good?

JOHN Yuwa. Gone. Travelling. Shifting through to the next stage of my journey. Travel to whatever place I'm headed next.

Silence.

JACK You already know where you going, unna?

JOHN Maybe.

DAVID I'm gonna miss ya, Dad.

JACK Yuwa.

JOHN — You boys have spent enough time missing ghosts. Stop being dickheads and be brothers again.

JOHN *hugs them both, placing a hand on each of their shoulders.*

JOHN — Now stop playing with ya nyanjis and make that call.

DAVID *nods and gets out his phone. He dials.*

DAVID — Mr Baldwin? Yeh we need to talk. The answer's no. The land's too important. Our marnta is too important. What I'm saying is, you go out there and do this, you can kiss your arse goodbye. No I mean it. Go out and sit with Elders and ask. There's protocols we need to follow. No. It's not enough. No. Brian, I'm telling you, no. There's too much in that area. Well get a survey together, talk to our old people and they'll take the boys out. Yeh I get it but YOU have to understand … Yeh. Ok, good. I'll make some calls next week. But Brian, I'm not promising anything. Alright. I'm turning my phone off. Catchya.

JOHN *sighs, deep relief.* DAVID *hangs up the phone and turns it off.* JACK *walks over and places a hand on his shoulder.*

JACK — I'm proud of you.

DAVID — You too. Sorry I've been dumb.

JACK — Nothing to be sorry for, you always dumb.

JACK *punches* DAVID *in the arm.*

DAVID Ya bloody frick.

A silence falls over the three.

JOHN David. I need to talk to Anne.

DAVID I'll come with you.

JOHN No. I have to talk to my daughter alone.

DAVID *nods.*

JACK And yaku?

JOHN I'll talk to her after. Need to work up the courage.

DAVID Well …

JACK Let's go grab a mayi.

DAVID Yuwa. Seeya Dad.

JACK Nyaku mama.

JOHN Love youse.

EXIT JACK *and* DAVID

SCENE SIXTEEN

BEDROOM

JOHN *walks over to* ANNE, *she stirs in her bed. Suddenly she wakes up, screams from shock.*

ANNE Holy shit! Who are you?

JOHN I'm John.

ANNE What are you doing in my room? Where's David? DAVID!

JOHN Aye, it's fine, everything is fine.

ANNE Wait. John? David's John? Aren't you … Dead?

JOHN Yuwa.

ANNE Am I dead?

JOHN No you're safe, everyone is.

ANNE Ah. Ok. Ok, ok, ok. Are you a ghost?

JOHN Kind of.

ANNE Mhmm mhmm, that's ok. Totally normal.

JOHN Hey, hey it's alright. I wanted to meet you before I go.

ANNE Go? Like move on, go?

He nods.

JOHN You a part of this family bub. The parna knows you now, it feels you. It'll watch you and little one. When she's old enough, it'll be her time.

ANNE Her? One less surprise … I don't understand. Why are you here now? How come I can see you?

JOHN I always came back around this time. Davie was too afraid to introduce me to you I guess. Not sure why …

ANNE This is pretty hectic. Not gonna lie.

Silence.

ANNE Well if you're going, will I see you again?

JOHN I don't think so.

ANNE I've just met you. I've got questions.

JOHN And Lilly has answers. I wish it could be me. I wish I could spoil my granny, take her out on country and teach her. I wish I could be there when you and Davie have your first dance. I wish I could be there for a lot of things, but I won't be. That's why I came. To see you, meet my daughter before I leave.

ANNE *hugs* JOHN, *he relaxes and hugs her back.*

JOHN Be strong, this parna is yours too now.

ANNE But … I'm white. Am I allowed to hear all this stuff?

JOHN Doesn't matter if you black, white or brindle, you family. You're my daughter, I'm tjamu for that little one in your tummy.

ANNE This is a lot.

JOHN It's ok bub, I understand. You got time to think, time to learn, it's just, I won't be the one to teach you.

ANNE Ok.

JOHN *nods and begins to laugh.*

JOHN Teach my boy how to dance please.

ANNE I will. Bye … Dad.

EXIT JOHN

ENTER DAVID

DAVID Anne?

ANNE Hey.

DAVID Are you ok?

ANNE Yeh I'm fine. Your dad came to see me.

BEAT

DAVID I didn't know how to tell you about him …

ANNE Well you should've given me the choice. It's not just you making decisions now.

DAVID *nods.*

DAVID You sure you're ok?

ANNE Yeh.

DAVID And bub?

ANNE SHE'S good.

DAVID She? Really?

ANNE *nods, beaming.*

DAVID I love you.

JOHN *begins to tap his tapping sticks.*

SCENE SEVENTEEN

KITCHEN

LILLY *is standing in the kitchen.*

ENTER JOHN

JOHN *reaches a hand out,* LILLY *eventually takes it. He pulls her into a hug.*

LILLY This isn't me.

JOHN No, it's not.

LILLY Then I need you to move on. Leave. Don't come back. Let me love, let me live. I don't want to be dead with you.

JOHN I never meant to hold you here, Lil. I've spent every moment watching you live in this pain, drown in it. Our love kept me strong in death, but it's been eating away at you. I was selfish, I've been selfish.

LILLY Don't be stupid.

LILLY *tears up.* JOHN *holds her face. She looks at him and they hug.*

LILLY The boys?

JOHN They'll be right.

LILLY And Anne?

JOHN She'll keep Davie doing the right thing.

They break apart.

LILLY This is really it.

JOHN It is.

They hug again, eventually letting go and looking at each other.

LILLY Seeya later, cowboy.

JOHN Bye, my desert princess.

JOHN *begins to tap his tapping sticks.*

ENTER DAVID, JACK *and* ANNE

JOHN *moves through the space, tapping his sticks.* ANNE, DAVID, JACK *and* LILLY *follow him to the frontyard.* JOHN *taps his sticks until he exits, the echo of tapsticks eventually fading in the distance. The family comes together, looking out into the distance.*

DAVID You right Mum?

LILLY Yeh I'm right.

DAVID *wraps an arm around* ANNE, *lights fade.*

SCENE EIGHTEEN

LILLY *sits at the kitchen humming and doing mindless work.* DAVID *packs clothes away in his bed, reflecting.*

ENTER ANNE

DAVID Hey.

ANNE Hey. You nearly done?

DAVID Yeh should be, plane not leaving for a couple hours right?

She sits and pats the bed.

DAVID Now? I think Mum's in the kitchen …

ANNE What? No I don't mean …

DAVID Muckin round.

He sits.

ANNE Your dad said I'm part of the family now. Deadly hey?

DAVID Dunno how I feel about you saying deadly.

ANNE C'mon we married up now.

DAVID Yukay, stop.

ANNE Sorry I'm just gammon.

DAVID Stop! Please, you're making my ancestors cry.

They sit.

ANNE Why didn't you tell me about him?

DAVID *reflects.*

DAVID I was scared. I wasn't ready to see him. For him to see me, who I turned into. I left this place and hardly looked back. Jack, Mum, our country, all of it. I left myself, my spirit.

ANNE Why would that stop you from introducing me to him though? I'm not you. I could've made my own opinions.

DAVID Yeh well, I wasn't thinking all that at the time.

ANNE Just don't forget hey. It's us, not you, making the decisions bossman.

DAVID Don't like that one.

He grabs her hand.

DAVID I love you.

ANNE I know you do.

She gets up and leaves the room.

DAVID Aye! You gotta say it back!

ANNE *blows a kiss and walks into the kitchen.* DAVID *finishes the packing.*

LILLY All packed?

ANNE Just about, David's just getting the last stuff packed.

LILLY Now, my girl, you had better look after yourself. Melbourne's pretty cold this time of year right?

ANNE We're stopping in Perth for a little bit, head home a bit later.

LILLY Might be time I hit the big city up hey, just for a holiday.

ANNE True! Come over, we'll have the spare bed ready whenever!

LILLY Could be nice to get out of the bush. Just for a little while, let these memories rest.

ENTER JACK

JACK Hey you mob ready? Plane's leaving soon.

DAVID Two hours you gudi!

JACK Take two hours to load your luggage princess.

DAVID *drags the luggage in.*

JACK Go on, boot's open.

EXIT DAVID

JACK Mum.

She is suspicious.

LILLY Yes ...?

JACK You gotta go see Mel tomorrow morning.

LILLY We made a deal my son! No seeing Mel until you—

She is cut off by the plane ticket that JACK *waves in her face.*

BEAT

LILLY I haven't got my glasses on, what is it?

JACK Truly? It's a plane ticket.

LILLY Aye? You actually leaving?

JACK Yuwa.

LILLY When?

JACK Now.

ANNE He's going to stay in Perth with us for a bit.

JACK David and me going on that survey with the mining mob so we'll be back in a fortnight.

LILLY Only going for two weeks?

JACK Yuwa, this my home Mum. I'm just gonna go spread my wings a little.

ENTER DAVID

DAVID That is our mother, don't talk that way in front of her.

LILLY So … It's going to be just me in the house.

The words hold weight.

DAVID Just you.

ANNE Will you be alright?

LILLY Of course. It'll give me some space. Time to process.

JACK Look I can stay if you need—

LILLY Don't be stupid! I finally got a chance to get your hairy cheeks out of here? I'll drop you off myself!

DAVID'S *alarm goes off.*

DAVID Check in's open … We better get going.

JACK Yuwa.

DAVID Love you Mum. You call me whenever you need ok?

LILLY I will.

ANNE And I'll send you those little alien pregnant photo things when we've got them.

JACK I'll be back soon.

LILLY Love you, all of you.

The group says final goodbyes. As they leave the house, we hear the car drive off down the road and then there is silence. LILLY *turns on the radio, Creedence Clearwater Revival's 'Up Around the Bend' plays.* LILLY *grabs a cup of tea and hums along, she eventually sits on* JOHN'S *chair, there is a tap stick then blackout.*

END

ORIGINAL CAST AND CREW

At The Blue Room Theatre:

JACK	Micah Kickett
DAVID	Zac James
ANNE	Caitlin Hampson
LILLY	Rayma Morrison
JOHN	Maitland Schnaars
DIRECTOR	Bruce Denny
STAGE MANAGER	Helah Milroy
PRODUCER	Emmanuelle Dodo-Balu
LIGHTING	Peter Young
SET AND COSTUME DESIGN	Bruce Denny
	Helah Milroy
PUBLICIST	Kaitlyn Commander
COMPOSERS	Steven Mccall
	David Richardson

Wimiya Woodley, Rayma Morrison performing Kangaroo Stew at Circuitwest: Jack and Lilly discuss David and Anne's arrival, photo by Dana Weeks Photography, 2022.

Zac James performing Kangaroo Stew at Circuitwest: David divulges plans for a new mine site, on sacred land, photo by Dana Weeks Photography, 2022.

Wimiya Woodley, Zac James: Jack and David perform Kantula, 'Dance Ceremony' during a Kangaroo Stew show at Circuitwest photo by Dana Weeks Photography, 2022.

Maitland Schnaars performing as John in Kangaroo Stew at Circuitwest: John teaches David a Tjukurpa (Dreaming) story, deep within the spirit realm. A stray spirit watches behind, photo by Dana Weeks Photography, 2022.

Zac James, Rayma Morrison at Circuitwest: David and Lilly prepare the table for dinner, it's Kangaroo Stew, photo by Dana Weeks Photography, 2022.

Maitland Schnaars, Zac James performing Kangaroo Stew at Circuitwest: John teaches David the origins of humanity, photo by Dana Weeks Photography, 2022.

ABOUT ZAC JAMES

Zac James is a Traditional Custodian, Wonguktha, Yamaji and Murri man. Having more than 15 years experience in the arts industry, he has crossed barriers, creating pathways for his community and others. He is a passionate change maker, advocate and speaker for his people and mob. A prolific playwright with eight plays having been professionally developed and performed as well as a screen actor (*8MMM Aboriginal Radio*, *Shadow Trackers*) and filmmaker (*Marlu Man*), his debut feature film entering production at the end of 2024. He has recently begun to make waves with his music project, MONGEEYA. His community work has been immense: previously the coordinator of the Theatrical Response Group at Constable Care Foundation, he delved into the realm of social work, taking these skills into his role as Creative Director at Yirra Yaakin Aboriginal Theatre Company where he developed a multitude of developmental and empowerment programs for disadvantaged youth around WA. This would lead him to become the state representative for ASSITEJ and eventually the national coordinator of an international delegation for Theatre Network Australia, representing Australia at Bibu, the international children's arts festival.

Compelling reads from Magabala Books

PRAISE FOR FIFO

"Confronting yet tempered with Aboriginal humour...FIFO is an important story that could justifiably be dedicated to the moguls of the mining industry."

Writing WA

PRAISE FOR FALSE CLAIMS OF COLONIAL THIEVES

"Country and land are separated by a schism of cultural practice and accumulated history ... Yet the beauty of this book is the courage to push on through pain and loss and see if an understanding of some sort is possible."

Dr Laurie Keim, Sydney Sun

PRAISE FOR ART

"The poetry in ART gains meaning with each read...
A thought-provoking collection."

Christian Alphonso, Books+Publishing

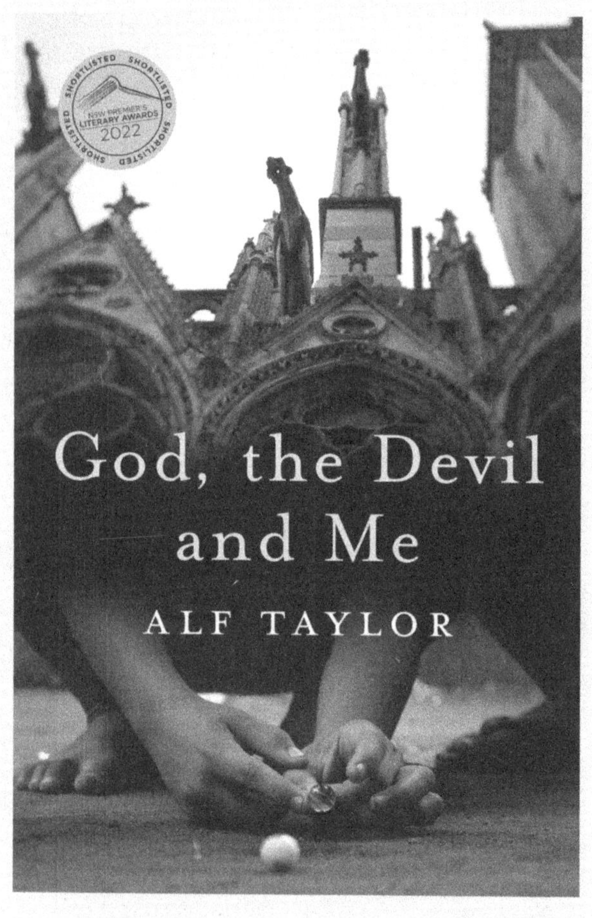

PRAISE FOR GOD, THE DEVIL AND ME

"Taylor has created a private universe...by turns incredibly sad and comic..."

Steven Carroll, The Sydney Morning Herald